# ONEPIECE

## Vol. 47
## CLOUDY, PARTLY BONY

STORY AND ART BY
**EIICHIRO ODA**

A musician swordsman whose shadow was stolen. He's on a quest to take it back.

**Brook**

Boundlessly optimistic and able to stretch like rubber, he is determined to become King of the Pirates.

**Monkey D. Luffy**

A former bounty hunter and master of the "three-sword" style. He aspires to be the world's greatest swordsman.

**Roronoa Zolo**

A thief who specializes in robbing pirates. Nami hates pirates, but Luffy convinced her to be his navigator.

**Nami**

A village boy with a talent for telling tall tales. His father, Yasopp, is a member of Shanks's crew.

**Usopp**

The bighearted cook (and ladies' man) whose dream is to find the legendary sea, the "All Blue."

**Sanji**

A blue-nosed man-reindeer and the ship's doctor.

**Tony Tony Chopper**

A mysterious woman in search of the Ponegliff on which true history is recorded.

**Nico Robin**

A softhearted cyborg and talented shipwright.

**Franky**

Monkey D. Luffy started out as just a kid with a dream—to become the greatest pirate in history! Stirred by the tales of pirate "Red-Haired" Shanks, Luffy vowed to become a pirate himself. That was before the enchanted Devil Fruit gave Luffy the power to stretch like rubber, at the cost of being unable to swim—a serious handicap for an aspiring sea dog. Undeterred, Luffy set out to sea and recruited some crewmates—master swordsman Zolo; treasure-hunting thief Nami; lying sharpshooter Usopp; the high-kicking chef Sanji; Chopper, the walkin' talkin' reindeer doctor; the mysterious archaeologist Robin; and cyborg shipwright Franky.

Luffy and crew have just directed their new vessel, the *Thousand Sunny*, toward Fish-Man Island on the Grand Line when they are caught in a storm and find themselves adrift in the perpetual fogs of the Florian Triangle. There they encounter Brook, a jovial skeleton with no shadow. When Brook reveals that he's a musician, Luffy tries to convince him to join the crew, but Brook cannot survive in the sunlight and turns down Luffy's invitation. Suddenly, the ship is pulled into the waters around Thriller Bark, a ghost island. The crew ends up heading ashore, where they encounter the prodigal physician Doctor Hogback, who's in the midst of creating an island full of zombies! Luffy finds out that one of the Seven Warlords of the Sea, Gecko Moria, is also on the island. As the bloodthirsty zombies gather for a Night Hunt, Gecko awakens…and the Straw Hats' fearsome night on Thriller Bark has just begun!!

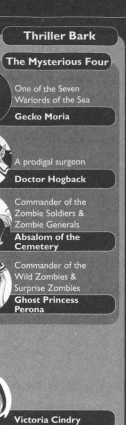

**Thriller Bark**

**The Mysterious Four**

One of the Seven Warlords of the Sea

**Gecko Moria**

A prodigal surgeon

**Doctor Hogback**

Commander of the Zombie Soldiers & Zombie Generals

**Absalom of the Cemetery**

Commander of the Wild Zombies & Surprise Zombies

**Ghost Princess Perona**

**Victoria Cindry**

**Hildon**

A pirate that Luffy idolizes. Shanks gave Luffy his trademark straw hat.

**"Red-Haired" Shanks**

## Vol. 47
## Cloudy, Partly Bony

## CONTENTS

# Chapter 450:
# NIGHT OF THE
# ZOMBIE GENERALS

**ENERU'S GREAT SPACE MISSION, VOL. 18:
"DR. TSUKIMI, MOON-GAZING CONNOISSEUR"**

USOPP'S BANNER READS: "EVIL SPIRITS BEGONE"--ED.

YOU WENT INSIDE THE ROOM?!

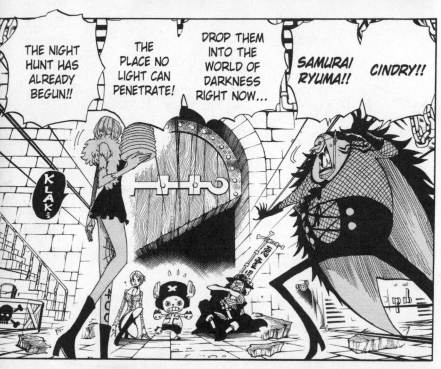

THE NIGHT HUNT HAS ALREADY BEGUN!!

THE PLACE NO LIGHT CAN PENETRATE!

DROP THEM INTO THE WORLD OF DARKNESS RIGHT NOW...

SAMURAI RYUMA!!

CINDRY!!

KLAK!!

YO HO HO!!

CHAK...

KACHAK...

?!

...‼

⁇‼

...

FWSH⋯

THREE-PACE HUM...

...ONLY AFTER THEY HAVE WALKED THREE STEPS, STILL HUMMING, SHALL THEY REALIZE THEY HAVE BEEN SLAIN.

THOSE WHO ARE SLAIN BY A MASTER...

WELL DONE! FO HO HO!

DOOM

FLUP FLUP...‼

KLANK‼

...NOTCH SLASH!!!

WE'RE COMING IN!!

THAT'S WAY TOO FAST!

KACHIK... KACHAKK!!

HUH? THIS DOOR'S LOCKED.

EXCUSE ME...

AND WHAT'S WITH THE MESS? IT'S LIKE SOMEONE HAD A FIGHT HERE.

MAYBE SOMETHING HAPPENED TO NAMI!

SUCH A HUGE MANSION AND THEY DON'T EVEN HAVE ONE SERVANT?

GECKO MORIA!

HELLO?! IS ANYONE HERE?!

DOOM!

HEY, NOW IT OPENS.

KRMBL...

KRIII...

YEAH, YOU OPENED IT...

HUH?

THERE'S A PIG GROWING OUT OF THE WALL.

YOU KNOW OF OUR MASTER...

...AND YET YOU STILL CAME. I APPLAUD YOUR COURAGE.

OINK OINK ...!!!

?!

GRAAH

BWA HA HA!!!

WELCOME, GUESTS!!

?!!!

WHOAA

NO CREATURE WE COME ACROSS ON THIS ISLAND WILL SURPRISE ME.

ARE THESE ALL ZOMBIES?

THEY'RE SLEEPING TIGHT IN THE BEDROOM RIGHT NOW. GOOD NEWS FOR YOU, RIGHT?

THEY'RE JUST FINE!

ABOUT THOSE OTHER THREE...

...WHERE'S THAT COOK WITH THE SPIRAL EYEBROWS?

HM? WAIT A SECOND...

WHA?

IT'S TRUE!! OINK! JUST GO AND SEE FOR YOURSELF!!

YOU'RE LYING.

RIGHT UP THOSE STAIRS! OINK OINK!

LOOKS LIKE THEY DID SOMETHING SNEAKY WHILE WE WEREN'T LOOKING.

OINK!

TEE HEE...

HEY, DON'T LAUGH! THEY'LL HEAR US!!

PFFT!!

...

WHERE DID SANJI GO?

HUH! HE WAS JUST HERE.

FIGHT TO YOUR HEART'S DESIRE TONIGHT!!!

OUR PREY HAS STEPPED WITHIN OUR BOUNDARIES!!

DOOM!!

...ZOMBIE GENERALS!!!

AWAKEN...

RMRMRM RM

ARISE, ANCIENT WARRIORS!!

KRII!!

KUNCH!

CHAK

Reader: When reading the Question Corner, please keep your room brightly lit and keep your face as far from the book as possible. Once finished reading, close your eyes and roll your eyeballs in all directions to keep them fit. (Oda, please be careful too!)

--Mr. Chu

Oda: Ahhh! There you are again! Trying to take over... Hm?! No, wait. After reading carefully, those are some kind and considerate words! Thank you so much for caring about everyone's health! I took a break last volume, so we'll put some extra ones in this time! Question Corner! Time to slart! (← I bit my tongue)

Q: What should I do if Eneru shoots his lightning at me?
--Pacchon, III

A: First, duck at the speed of light. Then do a corkscrew punch with your golden right arm! If that fails, cover your belly button✻ and run! He's strong, you know!

Q: Oda Sensei, I have a question! Please tell me the ages of the CP9 members. Please! Finger Pistol! (Sorry! Don't dodge it!)
--No. 1

A: Watch out!! Phew... That was close. I dodged! Hahaha! I'm not going to take it!

LUCCI 28　KAKU 23　JABRA 35　BLUENO 30　KUMADORI 34　FUKURŌ 29　KALIFA 25　SPANDAM 39

Q: Mr. Oda, I have a question. What happens when you pick your nose with the Finger Pistol? Please try it out.

--Prince

A: Sure. Ahhhhhhhhhhhhhhh!

*IN JAPANESE CULTURE, THERE IS A SUPERSTITION THAT ONE SHOULD COVER ONE'S BELLY BUTTON WHEN LIGHTNING STRIKES OR ELSE A LIGHTNING GOD WILL STEAL IT AWAY.--ED.

26

# Chapter 451:
# PERONA'S WONDER GARDEN

**ENERU'S GREAT SPACE MISSION, VOL. 19:
"THE MOON EXPLODED WHILE WE WERE MOON GAZING!"**

GROAAR!!!

YOU ZOMBIE GENERALS ARE STRONGER THAN ANYBODY!!!

KLANG

FIND AND CAPTURE THEM, WHEREVER THEY ARE!!

KLANG

KLANG KLANG

GEEZ, WHY IS HE LIKE THIS?

SLITHY...

HM? HURRY IT UP, CAPTAIN JOHN!

SHOW ME THAT YOU CAN LIVE UP TO THE INFAMY YOU ENJOYED WHILE STILL ALIVE.

OOF...

TWITCH!!

MASTER AB...♡

YEAH, YEAH. I'M GOING. HEH HEH!

THERE'S ALREADY A WOMAN I WANT TO MAKE MY BRIDE!!

THERE'S ALREADY...

HUFF

WAIT, LOLA!! LISTEN TO ME!!!

SHE'S STRONG-MINDED AND ELEGANT, BUT SHE IS A DELICATE, *LIVING* HUMAN!

HUFF

OH NO YOU DON'T.

I WON'T LET YOU TIE ME DOWN ANY LONGER!

SHE'S ONE OF THE PIRATES THAT ENTERED THE ISLAND. SHE'S BEAUTIFUL AND WOULD BE A PERFECT BRIDE FOR ME.

HMPH! YOU'LL NEVER BE HAPPY TOGETHER.

YOU FOOL! LOOK!

STOP! WAIT, LOLA!!

DASH!!

I'LL GO GET RID OF THAT WOMAN!!!

WAKE UP!

GET AHOLD OF YOURSELVES!!

HEY, USOPP!! NAMI!!

TWITCH TWITCH...

OOF...!!

...!!

THROB...

HE HIT US WITH THE BACK OF HIS SWORD!!

...THAT SAMURAI...

OW... HUH? I THOUGHT WE WERE...

JOLT

UGH...

THIS IS BAD! WE HAVE TO CALL FOR BACKUP!!

ALL THREE OF THEM WOKE UP!

ZWIP!!

IT'S A COFFIN!

...IN THIS BOX.

I DON'T KNOW, BUT I THINK THOSE SQUIRRELS WERE CARRYING US...

WE'RE OUTSIDE NOW...

IT MUST HAVE RAINED A LITTLE. THE GROUND IS WET.

YEEEK

LOOK! BEHIND US!!

WE WERE TAKEN PRETTY FAR AWAY.

WASN'T HOGBACK'S LAB ON THE TOP FLOOR?

THIS PLACE LOOKS LIKE THE BACK OF THE MANSION.

WHAT IS THAT...?! IT'S BEHIND THE MANSION!

?!!

THERE'S AN EVEN BIGGER BUILDING ON THE OTHER SIDE!!

DO

OM!!

I DIDN'T KNOW THERE WAS SUCH A HUGE BUILDING HERE!!!

...

WOOOO!

I FINALLY UNDERSTAND WHAT KIND OF PLACE THIS IS...

NAMI?!

SOMETHING DOESN'T ADD UP. WE WERE SCARED SILLY, AND WE RAN AROUND LIKE FOOLS...

WAIT A SECOND...

YEAH, LET'S START RUNNING RIGHT AWAY. BUT WHERE?

GOOD THING WE WOKE UP BEFORE THAT! LET'S RUN!

AFTER ALL IS SAID AND DONE...

THIS ROOM ISN'T THE TREASURE CHAMBER!

DO YOU REMEMBER WHAT THAT ZOMBIE SAID?

MY *SOMETHING'S FREAKY DETECTOR* IS DETECTING SOMETHING FREAKY!

WHAT ARE YOU TALKING ABOUT?!

...IS THAT ALL?

STOP THINKING ABOUT TRIVIAL STUFF! LET'S JUST GET OUT OF HERE!

AAH!!

DON'T SAY ANYTHING! LET'S JUST RUN, NAMI!

...I DON'T WANT TO RUN INTO THAT SAMURAI AGAIN.

I DON'T KNOW. IF WE GO BACK TO THE MANSION...

SO WHICH WAY DO YOU WANT TO RUN? FORWARD OR BACK?

THERE'S SOMETHING WRONG WITH YOUR EYES!

OF COURSE! I'M SCARED TOO!

BUT IF WE GO FORWARD, THERE MAY BE EVEN SCARIER THINGS AHEAD.

WHAAA!!

Q: Oda Sensei, I always enjoy reading *One Piece*. By the way, among the 200 captains and commanders that fought the Straw Hats in volume 44, wasn't there a Devil Fruit user that turned into a bunch of balls? What's the name and power of that Devil Fruit? It came up in the anime, but I couldn't make out what was being said. Oh, and please tell me about the Rust-Rust Fruit too.

--Mugi-Mugi

A: Regarding this, I've already announced it in a fanbook called *One Piece: Yellow*. But I'll tell it to anyone who doesn't have the book! During the battle, there were three Devil Fruit users.

 Captain Berry Good (Berry-Berry Fruit) A Grape Human

He can separate his body parts like grapes and rearrange himself into any shape he wants.

 Captain Shu (Rust-Rust Fruit) A Rust Human

Any metal he touches instantly rusts. He is the one who destroyed Zolo's sword, Yubashiri.

 Captain Sharingle (Wheel-Wheel Fruit) A Wheel Human

Each part of his body can spin like wheels. Able to perform high level attacks.

Q: Are those things on Kokoro's chest seashells? Or are they some sort of evolved scales? Or is it a "NuBra"?
--Lover of Old Ladies

A: Ugh... Ugh... *gasp*!! I'm sorry, I was having nightmares. What a question you've asked. Can I just say that I don't want to think about it? Oh, fine, I'll answer you. It's a "NuBra"-like thing. Its adhesive properties are second to none! Go, seashell "NuBra"!

BACK THE I NEVER THOUGHT.

46

# Chapter 452:
# JIGORO OF THE WIND

**ENERU'S GREAT SPACE MISSION, VOL. 20:
"TEARFUL DEPARTURE AFTER CHOKING ON A DUMPLING"**

IF YOU GET THROUGH THIS HALL, WE CAN GO TO THE COURTYARD OUTSIDE.

RIGHT. THIS ISN'T EVEN SUPPOSED TO BE THE FINAL BATTLE ANYWAY.

IT'S GOING TO TAKE TOO MUCH ENERGY TO FIGHT *ALL* OF THEM!!

ALL THOSE ATTACKS WERE INEFFECTIVE AGAINST ONE OF THEM.

GET THEM!!!

OKAY, THEN WE'LL MEET UP OVER THERE!

MAKE SURE NONE OF YOU DISAPPEAR AGAIN!!

HA! SURE...

LET'S GO!!!

LET ME OUT OF HERE!

?!

AHHHH!

KLUNK

HM?

CHNNNNG...!!

SWIP

OPEN THE LID! LET ME OUT!

LUFFY?!

WHAT? STRAW HAT IS IN THERE?!

WHAT'S THAT? A COFFIN?!

THAT VOICE!

TOMP

I WON'T LET YOU GO! OH OH OH...

?!

WE HAVE TO FOLLOW IT, NICO ROBIN!!

WHAT'S HE DOING? HE GOT CAUGHT?

Q: Oda Sensei, I have a question. In chapter 446 (volume 46), Chopper said that he's not interested in the bodies of human girls. Why?! He's supposed to be about 15 years old, right?! Chopper! Please ask him that!

--18 Year-Old Woman ♡

A: I see. Please read carefully. Chopper said that he's not interested in "human girls." He may be able to talk like humans, but Chopper is a reindeer. In other words, he may like people for their character, but their appearance can't excite him. But he might fall in love with a good-looking reindeer.

Q: Hello, Oda Sensei! I fell in love with Koby and Helmeppo when they reappeared in volume 45! They look too handsome! Tell me their birthdays! Koby should be May 13 (Bad Luck). And how about making Helmeppo's birthday July 16 (Freeloader)?

--Kukuri

A: You just answered your own question! Okay, we'll just leave it at that.

Q: Hello, Oda Sensei. ♡ *mumble mumble* (Sounds of the audience). By the way, there is suspicion that Koby has undergone full body cosmetic surgery at the Oda Clinic. Please comment! (Hands over two mics) I hope Koby can comment on this too.

--OP-Loving Saitama-Dwelling Wakayama-Living Mayuko

A: He's having a growth spurt! Just like those boys who grow a tremendous amount during summer vacation! He just burned off all the fat! Right, Koby?!

KOBY: Yup!

# Chapter 453:
# CLOUDY, PARTLY BONY

**ENERU'S GREAT SPACE MISSION, VOL. 21:
"TO THE MOON!"**

THRILLER BARK PERONA'S WONDER GARDEN

RM RM RM RM RM

WOOOOO

WE ZOMBIES SHOULDN'T BE ABLE TO GO AGAINST THE ORDERS OF OUR MASTER!!

HEY! WHAT DO YOU THINK YOU'RE DOING, NEWCOMER?!

PLUS, HE'S AS STRONG AS A ZOMBIE GENERAL!

DOOM

WHY IS HE ABLE TO?!

THE NAME OF THAT TEMPEST IS...

...LOVE!!!

A POWER THAT CAN'T BE MEASURED! A POWER THAT MAKES THE IMPOSSIBLE POSSIBLE! A POWER THAT BLOWS EVERYTHING AWAY!

AHH! HE'S OUR ENEMY AFTER ALL!

SHUT YOUR TRAP, YOU DARNED DIRTY PIRATES!

HEY, INU-PENG! DO YOU KNOW SANJI?!

WE'RE SANJI'S BUDDIES, SO YOU SHOULD HELP US...

...JUST LIKE SANJI!

I KNEW IT! THAT DOG-PENGUIN IS SAYING STUPID THINGS...

WAIT, LOLA!!!

I HEAR SOMETHING IN THE DISTANCE! WHAT IS IT NOW?!

WAIT!!

TMP TMP TMP

TMP TMP TMP...

HM?

YOU CAN TELL HE'S NOT NORMAL JUST BY LOOKING AT HIM! LET'S HURRY!!

W-WHAT'S GOING ON? HE'S STILL STANDING!

IT'S LIKE I'VE BEEN STRUCK BY LIGHTNING!

KRAKL KRAKL

WHAT IS THIS...THIS SHOCK THAT RUNS THROUGH MY ENTIRE BODY?!

YOU'RE NOT GETTING AWAY, YOU CAT BURGLAR HOME-WRECKER!!!

...LOVE ?!!

DOOM!!

IS THIS...

FWOOM!!

BUT WHY DID I EVEN TRY TO PROTECT HER?!

OH, NO! THAT LADY WILL BE ATTACKED!

WOBBL...

MY BODY WON'T MOVE LIKE IT'S SUPPOSED TO! THIS BODY IS TOO WEAK!!

THAT'S RIGHT! MISTRESS PERONA'S PUNISHMENTS WILL BE WAITING FOR US IF WE SCREW UP!

IT'S OUR JOB TO CATCH THOSE THREE!

H-HEY! WE BETTER GET MOVING!

HUPP...!!!

...

WHAT ARE YOU...

SHUSH!!

DON'T MAKE ABSALOM MAD!!

HEY, NEWCOMER! STOP IT!

...THAT LADY!

I WON'T LET YOU GO AFTER...

FWIP...

...

BOOM!!!

!!!

ARGH!!

AHHH!

FLOP...!!

...!!

SHIVSHIV...

GULP...!

KRAKKRAK

KRASH!!

WAIT!

YOU WANT TO USE ME AS A DECOY?! HEARTLESS JERK!!

WANNA SPLIT UP?!

HEY, NAMI! YOU'RE ALWAYS THE ONE THEY'RE AFTER!

TMP TMP TMP

SMASH

THAT BOAR IS SCARY!!

YEAH, TELL ME ABOUT IT!

...CAN SEE THROUGH ANYTHING YOU DO!

OH OH OH OH! MISTRESS PERONA'S GHOST NETWORK...

...BUT THE GIANT SPIDER WEB THAT CAUGHT *SUNNY* WAS YOUR WORK, WASN'T IT?

I DON'T KNOW IF YOU'RE AN IDIOT SPIDER OR AN IDIOT MONKEY...

*KLANG...*

*KLANG...*

*KLANG...*

*THEY'RE JUST FOR SHOW?!*

EXCUSE ME, WHAT?

THOSE LARGE EARS OF YOURS MUST BE USEFUL...

...FOR GATHERING INFORMATION.

I'LL TRY TO FOLLOW YOUR LEAD.

AS YOU WISH.

COUP DE...

SOUNDS LIKE A PLAN.

LET'S DO IT.

I'LL NEED TO TAKE ACTION, QUICK...

THE SITUATION IS HOPELESS! COMPLETELY SURROUNDED, AS THEY SAY.

*KLANG*

...YOU WANT TO LEAVE IT TO ME?

CHANK

WHAAAAT
?!!

?!!

**BO**

YOU DESTROYED
THE CONNECTING
PASSAGEWAY!!!

KRASH

SMASH.!!

AHHH!

W A A A A A H...

CIEN
FLEURS
...

RMRMRM

RMRMRM

FLAP!!

...WING!!!

DO OM!!!

WHOA!!

YOU CAN FLY?!!

FLAP

FLAP

YOU...

FLAP...

WHAT...?!

NO, THAT'S MORE THAN ENOUGH TIME!!

CHAKA!

...WAY TOO SHORT!!

DO OM!!!

FOR ABOUT FIVE SECONDS.

...!!

RMB..

KRENK..

KR A K K A !!

OOF!

I'M SURE THIS ISN'T THE END OF IT...

...BUT THEY WON'T COME AFTER US FOR A WHILE.

...

EVERYONE FELL DOWN TO THE COURTYARD.

HUFF...

...!!

HUFF...

WHY, YOU...!!

BRMB!!

I'M A SPIDER! I'LL SCURRY UP TO YOU RIGHT AWAY!

HEY! YOU STEPPED ON ME TO JUMP UP THERE!!

EVERY-THING WENT ALL RIGHT.

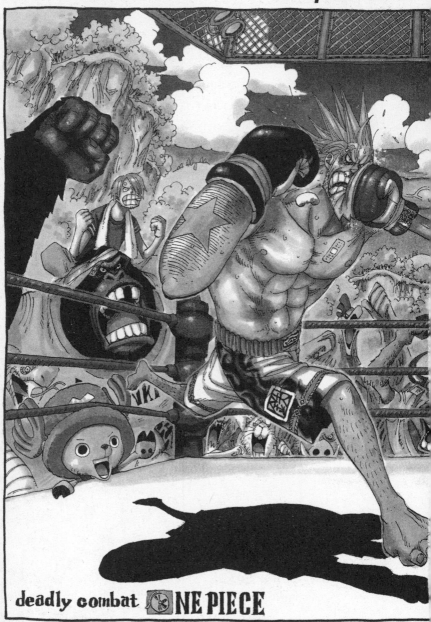

deadly combat ONE PIECE

# THE HUMMING SWORDSMAN

WHAT IS THAT?!

! WHAT'S THAT?

A A A A A HA A A

HUH...?

HM?

HM?

KRMB...

DO

A A A A A

SOMETHING ...NO, SOMEONE IS FALLING...

HA HA

...FROM THE SKY!!!

BECAUSE I'M A SKELETON!!

BOOM!!

BONE!!

COME ON, NOW.

WHAAAT?!

WHOA!!

WHAAT?!!

WHOA!

WHAT?! REALLY?!

REALLY! NO JOKE!

DOOM!!

...I THINK YOU AND THAT BEAST-MAN WILL MAKE A GREAT COUPLE! I'M ROOTING FOR YOU!!

R-REALLY?

THAT'S RIGHT! I'M A CROSS-DRESSER! NO JOKE!

BESIDES...

F-FRIEND-SHIP...

THAT'S WHAT FRIENDSHIP IS ALL ABOUT! MY NAME IS *NAMIZO*. CALL ME NAMI FOR SHORT.

PULL YOUR FACE UP, MY FRIEND!

GRIN

SHE TAMED IT...

NO ONE HAS EVER ENCOURAGED THIS LOVE OF MINE...

KLUNK

KLUNK

YOU'RE THE FIRST PERSON TO OFFER ME SUCH KIND WORDS.

A LOOPHOLE! A ROTTEN LOGICAL LOOPHOLE!

LOLA, YOU'RE A ZOMBIE.

ATTACK HIM IN HIS SLEEP? IS THAT OKAY, LIKE, ETHICALLY? FOR A HUMAN BEING?!

THAT'S WHY YOU NEED TO GET HIM IN HIS SLEEP.

YOU KNOW, HE'S NOT GOING TO GIVE YOU THE THUMBPRINT IF HE'S CONSCIOUS.

EVEN IF HE'S NOT ASLEEP, YOU CAN KNOCK HIM UNCONSCIOUS FIRST.

HEY, NAMIZO, DON'T YOU WANT TO RUN AWAY?

EVEN WHEN SHE FALLS, SHE WON'T GET UP WITHOUT A PRICE.

OH, YOU'RE SO SILLY. THAT PLACE IS CLOSE TO MISTRESS PERONA'S ROOM.

SO NAMI WAS REALLY A MAN...

...BUT I DON'T REMEMBER WHERE IT IS. CAN YOU TELL ME HOW TO GET THERE?

BY THE WAY, LOLA, I LOST SOMETHING AT THE TREASURE STORAGE. I WANT TO GO BACK AND GET IT...

REALLY?!

TMP TMP TMP TMP

HEY, NAMI! HE'S BACK!

!!

...

YAK YAK

NO WONDER SHE SEEMED SO MANLY.

THEY JUST HAVE SOME MONEY.

THEY HAVE BOXES, BUT THEY'RE ALL EMPTY.

...ON THIS SHIP?

THEY DON'T EVEN HAVE ONE TREASURE CHEST...

THOUSAND SUNNY AT THRILLER BARK

YES, MA'AM.

WHATEVER... THEY SEEM TO HAVE LOTS OF FOOD, SO LET'S TAKE THAT FOR NOW.

BUMP BUMP

MISTRESS PERONA!

IS THIS REALLY THE SHIP SAILED BY THE MAN WHO DEFEATED CROCODILE?

...THEY'VE HARDLY GOT ANYTHING OF VALUE.

WHAT A WASTE OF TIME. WITH BOTH THEIR SHIPS COMBINED...

AND THEY WILL REVEAL NUMBER 900!

THEY HAVE CAPTURED LUFFY THE STRAW HAT!

MASTER IS? WHY?

MASTER MORIA IS CALLING FOR THE MYSTERIOUS THREE.

HILDON.

NUMBER 900?! REALLY?!

21

FLAP FLAP FLAP

ABSALOM, YOU DIRTY BEAST! COME OUT HERE AND MARRY ME!!

ROOOAR!!!!!

MASTER AB!!!

YOU DISAPPEARED AGAIN, DIDN'T YOU?!

WAIT. MY BUSINESS FIRST! DID THREE PIRATES GO YOUR WAY?

BIG TROUBLE!

OH! OH, SIR ABSALOM! WE HAVE TROUBLE!

HEY, KUMACY.

THAT'S ODD...

OH. OH, ABOUT THAT...

KLAK KLAK

THERE'S NO OTHER PLACE TO RUN.

BUT I HAVE SOMETHING IMPORTANT TO...

STOP TALKING, KUMACY! HOW MANY TIMES DO I HAVE TO TELL YOU THAT?!

W- WELCOME BACK, MISTRESS PERONA!

WHAT ARE YOU DOING HERE?! THIS IS MY ROOM!

ABSALOM!

SHUT UP!! DON'T MAKE A SOUND!

PERONA.

SOMEONE FELL FROM THE SKY!

RM RM RM RM RM RM RM---

SIZZZ...

COULD IT BE...

WHAT FELL?

?

SIZZZ...

I HAVE A PRETTY GOOD IDEA WHO IT IS.

NO, WAIT.

RM RM

RM RM...

Q: This may be sudden, but in chapter 412 of volume 43, Nami was tearing off Kalifa's clothes looking for the key... but isn't that going a bit too far?! Right in front of Franky too! It's sexual harassment! No one will want to marry her now! Mr. Oda, can I have Kalifa?!

--"I Would Die For A Secretary Like That"

A: Ready, and... You want her?!

Q: Oda Sensei, is it true that half of you is composed of smut?

--Scenic Traveler

A: Yes. Well, the other half is made of stupidity. I'm not really worth anything alive, but even if aliens from outer space were to attack earth and destroy the world, I have the utmost confidence that I will survive.

Q: Oda! My older brother tells me that the comics in *Jump* magazine run in the order of their popularity. Is that true?!

--Yasumo

A: That's a good question from a Jump reader. I get these questions quite often. Actually that's not exactly how it works: The Jump publication's deputy editor-in-chief chooses the order every week... but of course, the popular ones do have a tendency to run in the front. That vice editor-in-chief promotes certain comics on certain weeks depending on the mood. To be specific, the order is intended to "maximize the enjoyment of the reading public." But it's up to you to read it in whatever order you want.

Q: Isn't the Bubble-Bubble Fruit that Kalifa ate more of a Logia type than a Paramythia type?

--Fruit Punch Samurai

A: Kalifa has bubbles coming from her. The actual shape of her body doesn't change, so it's a Paramythia type. Rub and bubbles come out. Isn't that convenient?

# Chapter 455:
# GECKO MORIA OF THE SEVEN WARLORDS OF THE SEA

ENERU'S GREAT SPACE MISSION, VOL. 22:
"HE WHO KILLED THE DOCTOR: A MAN'S GOTTA DO WHAT
A MAN'S GOTTA DO!"

EVEN AFTER BEING CUT DOWN, THE ZOMBIES KEEP GETTING BACK UP.

WE'RE NOT DONE YET...

AAAH!!

HM? WAIT! I'VE SEEN YOU SOMEWHERE BEFORE.

RMRMRMRMRM...

WHY, YOU...

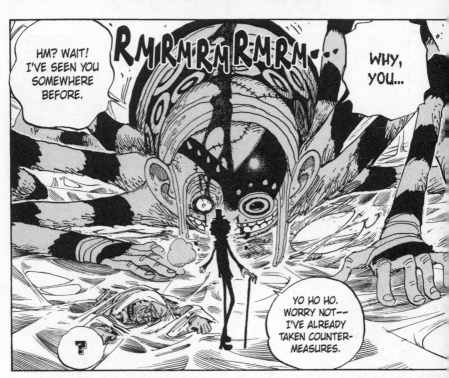

YO HO HO. WORRY NOT-- I'VE ALREADY TAKEN COUNTER-MEASURES.

AHHH!! AH!

THE ZOMBIES HAVE A CERTAIN WEAKNESS...

COUNTER-MEASURES?

WHAT IS *THAT*?!

Ss... KK AHHHHH!!

NOW, RETURN TO YOUR ORIGINAL MASTER!

FWOOO...

AHHH! AHHH!

THAT'S THE ZOMBIE'S SOUL!

SOUL?! I CAN SEE IT COMING OUT!

NOOO! CAPTAIN TARALAN!

CAPTAIN! CAPTAIN WAS DEFEATED!

WHU

THAT'S THE MAN WHO MADE A MESS OF THRILLER BARK FIVE YEARS AGO!

LOOK! IT'S THE **HUMMING SWORDSMAN!**

I PURIFIED IT.

YOU REALLY KNOCKED IT OUT FOR GOOD. WHAT DID YOU DO?

...

YOU'RE RIGHT! IT'S MELTING!

OH, AND THOSE SPIDER WEBS ARE RESISTANT TO STRENGTH BUT VULNERABLE TO FIRE.

...?

WE HAVE TO REPORT THIS TO MASTER!

FWOOF!!

SIZZ...!!

RSTL

RSTL

RSTL

IF THEY WERE CAPTURED, IT MAY ALREADY BE TOO LATE.

YES. BUT I DON'T KNOW WHERE TO START.

YOU SEEM TO KNOW A LOT ABOUT THIS ISLAND.

STRAW HAT AND THE OTHERS WERE TAKEN AWAY!

WHAT DO YOU MEAN "TOO LATE" ?!!

STOP IT. HE'S ALREADY DEAD.

...!!!

YO HO HO! GET IT?! ANOTHER SKULL JOKE!

BUT I'M A SKELETON, SO I DON'T HAVE A FACE!

HEE HEE!!

CHAK!!

P-PLEASE DON'T SHOUT AT ME IN PUBLIC LIKE THAT...

I MIGHT LOSE FACE!

...ON A SHIP THAT COULDN'T BE STEERED.

AS I TOLD YOU BEFORE, I WANDERED THE SEAS FOR DECADES...

STOP IT. HE'S ALREADY DEAD.

...!!!

ANYWAY, SERIOUSLY... PLEASE LISTEN TO ME.

IRK!!

CHAK!!

MUCH IN THE SAME WAY YOU DID.

...I ARRIVED AT THRILLER BARK FIVE YEARS AGO.

AND THAT'S HOW...

...THE RUDDER WAS BROKEN, SO I HAD TO JUST LET THE CURRENTS CARRY ME.

THOUGH I WANTED TO ESCAPE THESE DEMONIC WATERS...

BUT ALL I FOUND WERE MONSTERS AND ZOMBIES.

...AND EXPLORED THE PLACE ON FOOT.

...I STARTED SEARCHING FOR PARTS TO FIX THE RUDDER...

BECAUSE I WANTED TO ESCAPE FROM THE FLORIAN TRIANGLE...

GHOSTS!!

I WAS EVENTUALLY CAPTURED AND TAKEN TO THIS BUILDING.

...AND A PATCHED-UP CORPSE THEY CALLED A MARIONETTE.

...WAS A MARTIAL ARTS DANCER...

WHAT I WITNESSED INSIDE...

...

...AND REMOVED!

THE MARTIAL ARTIST'S SHADOW WAS PULLED FROM THE GROUND...

?!

THEN A LARGE MAN APPEARED, AND WHAT I SAW NEXT STRUCK FEAR IN MY HEART.

I'M GOING TO BEAT YOU UP IF YOU DON'T QUIT JOKING!!

EVEN THOUGH I DON'T HAVE ANY EYES!!!

I DOUBTED MY EYES TOO, AT FIRST.

HE CUT OFF THE SHADOW?

YES, GO AHEAD AND BEAT HIM UP.

YOHOHO

WHAT DO YOU THINK HAPPENED NEXT?

...INSIDE THE LIFELESS MARIONETTE.

AND THE SHADOW ITSELF WAS PRESSED...

...I SAW THE MAN COLLAPSE AFTER HIS SHADOW WAS TAKEN.

I WOULD SOON SUFFER THE SAME FATE, BUT FIRST...

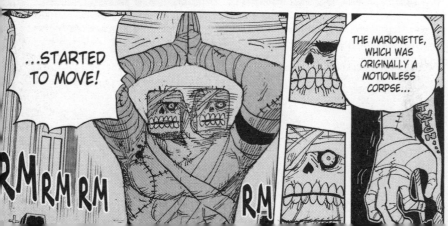

...STARTED TO MOVE!

THE MARIONETTE, WHICH WAS ORIGINALLY A MOTIONLESS CORPSE...

RMRMRM

RM

TWITCH

UNDER NORMAL CIRCUMSTANCES...

THE SHADOW AT YOUR FEET IS THE SAME.

THE SHADOW IS ANOTHER SOUL THAT FOLLOWS ITS MASTER'S MOVES.

WHAT DO YOU MEAN?!

...IS ONE OF THE SEVEN WARLORDS... *GECKO MORIA!*

HE HAS THE POWER OF THE SHADOW-SHADOW FRUIT.

THE MAN WHO IS ABLE TO CAPTURE AND FORCE THOSE SHADOWS TO SUBMIT TO HIM...

...THAT SOUL IS SUPPOSED TO FOLLOW YOU FROM BIRTH TO DEATH.

...

THE PROBLEM HERE IS THAT HE'S WORKING WITH A TALENTED SURGEON WHO CAN BUILD POWERFUL CORPSES USING THE BODY PARTS OF VARIOUS CREATURES.

AS LONG AS DR. HOGBACK IS ON GECKO MORIA'S SIDE, OUR TROUBLES HAVE NO END.

...AND CREATE ZOMBIES.

AS LONG AS HE HAS THE CORPSES TO USE, HE CAN MANIPULATE SHADOWS...

A DEVIL FRUIT.

THERE ARE STILL A HUGE NUMBER OF MARIONETTES, PRESERVED...

...IN HIS LABORATORY FREEZER.

...AND REVIVE THE BODIES OF LEGENDARY WARRIORS.

HIS MEDICAL SKILLS MAKE IT POSSIBLE FOR HIM TO GO TO VARIOUS CEMETERIES...

...THOUGH THE PHYSICAL STRENGTH WILL BE DEPENDENT ON THE BODY OF THE MARIONETTE.

THE PERSONALITY AND BATTLE ABILITIES ARE RETAINED FROM THE ORIGINAL OWNER OF THE SHADOW...

DR. HOGBACK... I DIDN'T REALIZE THAT AFTER HE WENT MISSING...

...THE FAMOUS PHYSICIAN CAME HERE TO WORK FOR A PIRATE.

...BUT THAT DOESN'T MEAN THE DEAD HAVE ACTUALLY COME BACK TO LIFE.

SO WHAT YOU'RE SAYING IS THAT THE ZOMBIES CAN MOVE AROUND...

THAT'S WHY MORIA SEEKS OUT THE SHADOWS OF PEOPLE WITH BOUNTIES ON THEIR HEADS... IT MAKES THINGS EASIER.

...THE MORE POWERFUL THE ZOMBIE SOLDIER WILL BE.

THE STRONGER THE COMBINATION OF THE PHYSICAL BODY AND SHADOW WARRIOR IS...

CORRECT.

TO MORIA, THE OVERWHELMING BENEFIT OF USING ZOMBIES IS LIKELY THEIR OBEDIENCE.

SO THAT'S WHAT THRILLER BARK REALLY IS.

...HE'S AFTER US.

I GET IT. SO THAT'S WHY...

USUALLY THE POWER OF A WARRIOR IS DIRECTLY PROPORTIONAL TO HOW DIFFICULT IT IS TO CONTROL THEM.

THE STRONGER THEY ARE, THE MORE QUICKLY THEY ARE SENT BACK OUT TO SEA WHILE STILL UNCONSCIOUS.

...HE HAS NO NEED FOR THE ORIGINAL OWNER OF THE SHADOW.

?!!

YES. AFTER TAKING A SHADOW THAT HAS THE SAME BATTLE ABILITIES AS THE ACTUAL PERSON...

...PLEASE TRUST ME AND DO AS I SAY!

I WILL EXPLAIN THE BEST PLAN OF ACTION...

IT'S ALL RIGHT. WE STILL HAVE TIME.

WHAT?! THEN THEY'RE IN TROUBLE!

WE'RE LISTENING. HURRY UP AND TALK.

IT'S SO FUN!

GET IT?! I HAVEN'T HAD THIS KIND OF AUDIENCE IN DECADES!!

YOHOHO

YOU'D HAVE TO BE OUT OF YOUR SKULL!!

WHAT?! TRUST *YOU*?!

RM RM RM RM

TROMP...

RM RM RM

YES, MA'AM.

RM RM

THAT WAS FAST. COME IN!

THE MYSTERIOUS THREE HAVE ALL COME TOGETHER!

MASTER!!

TROMP

TROMP

ONE IS ZOLO THE PIRATE HUNTER...

...AND THE OTHER IS A BLOND MAN WITH NO BOUNTY.

HEY, STRAW HAT LUFFY. YOU SEEM TO HAVE MADE A NAME FOR YOURSELF...

...BUT YOU'RE THE THIRD I'VE CAPTURED SO FAR.

I DON'T KNOW WHO THESE PEOPLE ARE, BUT THIS IS GETTING REALLY BAD!

WHY ARE THE THREE STRONGEST GUYS THE FIRST TO GET CAUGHT?!

WHAT? HEY, ZOLO AND SANJI GOT CAPTURED!

WHSP WHSP

I-IT CAN'T BE! LUFFY IS CAPTURED NOW TOO!

HUH? BLOND? ONLY SANJI'S BLOND.

UM... UM...

MAYBE THEY GOT AWAY.

KUMACY NEVER RECEIVED THEM.

WHAT HAPPENED TO THOSE THREE, PERONA?!

I THOUGHT I HAD THE RISKY BROTHERS DELIVER THEM TO YOU.

SHUT UP! YOU BETTER NOT TELL THEM!

HE'S TALKING ABOUT US!

HM? WAIT A SECOND.

BUT THOSE THREE, INCLUDING MY BRIDE, WERE CAUSING TROUBLE AT THE COURTYARD.

YOU'RE WAY TOO STRICT ON KUMACY.

I SAID, SHUT YOUR MOUTH!

UNBEARABLY STRICT

OH...

HEY, CINDRY! YOU'RE JUST MAKING THINGS WORSE!

WHAT ARE YOU SAYING, CINDRY?!

NO ONE WILL EVER MARRY YOU.

GROWR!!

THAT MEANS... HOGBACK!!

AND WHY ARE YOU STANDING IN FRONT OF ME?!

DOOM

...NOT TO...

YOU HURT MY WIFE! EVEN AFTER I TOLD YOU...

IF THE PIRATES ESCAPED, YOU ALL HAVE TO DO SOMETHING ABOUT IT!

STOP IT, ALL OF YOU! YOU'RE ANNOYING ME.

GRAH

GRAH

AGH! I GOT HIT BY A STRAY BULLET!!

NO ONE WILL EVER MARRY YOU, EITHER.

DOOM

Q: I have a question. In chapters 436 to 437 (volume 45), there is a wealthy-looking girl holding a pair of binoculars. What is she looking at? Franky may be a pervert, but I think she is too. I want to know her name and what she's like, so please tell me! And keep up the good work!

--Gengerous Zone

A: So you found her. I see. Then let me announce it! Her name is Marmieta (I can see everything). And the person next to her is the Butler, Yamenahare (Please stop it). She is the only daughter of the mayor, Bimine (How tasty), of Pucci, the Gourmet City, which is connected to Water Seven via the Sea Train. Though she is very naïve, she's curious about everything. After she heard of the damages Aqua Laguna caused, she went to Water Seven to deliver relief goods. But there she saw a very strange sight!

Q: I've been wondering this for a very long time, but did you model Robin off of... me?!

--Nico Aya

A: Yeah, whatever.

Q: Hey, Oda Sensei! I've been wondering about this... In volume 45, Robin grabbed Franky. Can Robin feel what she's grabbing? Please tell me!

A: Yes, she can. All the appendages she sprouts are a part of her body. So she can feel everything those sprouted appendages touch, and if they get hurt, she gets hurt, too. In that circumstance, it was like she grabbed Franky with her bare hands! Girls, please don't do stuff like this.

# Chapter 456:
# DEMON FROM THE LAND OF ICE

**ENERU'S GREAT SPACE MISSION, VOL. 23:
"ULTIMATE MORTIFICATION! THE SPACE PIRATE WAS TOO STRONG"**

YOU WANT US TO GO BACK TO SUNNY?!

GO BACK TO THE SHIP?!

BUT JUST BECAUSE THEIR SHADOWS HAVE BEEN TAKEN, IT DOESN'T MEAN THEY'LL DIE.

...IS TO HAVE THEIR SHADOWS TAKEN AWAY!

THE WORST POSSIBLE SITUATION FOR THE CAPTURED CREWMEMBERS...

THAT'S RIGHT.

LIKE ME, FOR EXAMPLE!

CORRECT! BUT RIGHT WHEN YOUR SHADOW IS TAKEN AWAY, YOU LOSE CONSCIOUSNESS ON THE SPOT...

SO WE WON'T DIE EVEN IF OUR SHADOWS ARE TAKEN AWAY.

THIS SITUATION HAS NOTHING TO DO WITH THAT!!

OH WAIT, I AM DEAD!! GET IT?!!

...AND YOU DON'T WAKE UP FOR AT LEAST TWO DAYS.

TO PREVENT THE VICTIMS FROM COMING BACK TO THE ISLAND, PERHAPS?

THAT'S RIGHT!

DO YOU UNDERSTAND WHY THEY WOULD DO THAT?

THE STRONGER THE PERSON IS, THE MORE LIKELY IT IS THEY'LL BE PUT ON A SHIP AND EJECTED FROM THRILLER BARK.

...

THIS IS IMPORTANT. PLEASE LISTEN CAREFULLY.

THEY CAN'T!

THEN WHY DON'T THEY JUST KILL THE VICTIM WHILE THEY'RE PASSED OUT?

THE ENEMY DOESN'T WANT THIS TO HAPPEN, SO THEY ALWAYS KEEP THE ORIGINAL ALIVE.

BASICALLY, THE ZOMBIE WILL DIE AT THE SAME TIME!

IF THE ORIGINAL DIES, THEN THE SHADOW WILL VANISH AS WELL.

THE ORIGINAL AND THE SHADOW ARE A PART OF THE SAME PERSON.

ZOMBIE

SHADOW

ORIGINAL OWNER

...THAT WOULD BE THE WORST POSSIBLE STATE OF AFFAIRS! YOU'D ALL LOSE YOUR SHADOWS AND END UP HAVING TO WANDER THE SEAS!

NOW IF YOU TWO FALL VICTIM AS WELL...

...THEY WILL DEFINITELY BE ALIVE AND ON THEIR WAY BACK TO THE SHIP!

SO EVEN IF YOUR CREWMATES' SHADOWS WERE TAKEN...

...

THAT IS THE ONLY WAY YOU'LL HAVE A CHANCE TO RETAKE THE SHADOWS!

THE BEST THING YOU CAN DO IS WAKE UP THE ONES WHO ARE SLEEPING.

YOU JUST SAW HOW EFFECTIVE IT WAS AGAINST THE SPIDER MONKEY.

IT'S THE ZOMBIES' WEAKNESS.

THEIR WEAKNESS! WHAT IS IT?!

WHAT?

AND HERE-- TAKE THIS.

I SEE. MAKES SENSE TO ME.

SALT...?!

SALT.

IS IT A CHARM TO WARD OFF EVIL SPIRITS OR SOMETHING?

SINCE SALT EMBODIES THE POWER OF THE OCEAN...

...THE BODY AND ITS FAKE SOUL WILL NOT BE ABLE TO MAINTAIN A BOND.

WELL, IT'S SOMETHING LIKE THAT.

THE ZOMBIES ARE ABLE TO MOVE DUE TO THE POWERS OF THE DEVIL FRUIT.

IT'S SIMPLE--TO DEFEAT THE ZOMBIES, JUST PUT SALT IN THEIR MOUTHS.

GET IT?!

BONES!

THERE. I MADE NO BONES ABOUT IT!

I DIDN'T KNOW THEY HAD THAT WEAKNESS.

I SEE. SO THE THING THAT THE MONKEY SPAT OUT...

...WAS THE SHADOW THAT WAS INSIDE IT.

I WAS DRIFTING AWAY ON MY SHIP, BUT LUCKILY I WOKE UP WITH ENOUGH TIME TO TURN BACK.

SO I RETURNED TO THE ISLAND AND FOUGHT, WHICH RESULTED IN UTTER DEFEAT!

MY SHADOW WAS TAKEN FROM ME FIVE YEARS AGO.

NO BONES!! HA!

BUT HOW DO YOU KNOW SO MUCH ABOUT THE ZOMBIES ON THIS ISLAND?

...SO I MUST ESCAPE THESE DEMONIC WATERS...

...AND FULFILL THE PACT I MADE WITH A FRIEND. THAT IS WHY I RAN TO SAVE MY LIFE!

I FLED BECAUSE I FEARED FOR MY LIFE. I JUST DID NOT WANT TO DIE.

I AM THE LAST SURVIVOR FROM MY SHIP...

I WILL DEFEAT THAT MAN AND TAKE BACK MY SHADOW!!

THAT'S WHY I WILL NOT RUN AWAY THIS TIME!!!

THOUGH I SURVIVED, IT DIDN'T SOLVE ANYTHING.

...

....!!!

...?!

WAIT A SECOND!!

I MUST HURRY ON MY WAY!

NOW, IF YOU'LL EXCUSE ME!

...BEFORE YOU GO.

YOU MIGHT AS WELL ANSWER...

...ONE MORE QUESTION...

RM RM RM

RM...

WHAT WAS THAT? DID YOU SEE THAT?!

IT WAS HIS SHADOW! HIS SHADOW GOT CUT OFF!

LUFFY!!

KUMACY! WHAT ARE YOU MUMBLING ABOUT NOW?!

HM?

AAAH!

YOU'RE WAY TOO STRICT ON KUMACY.

OH... OH...

I DON'T BELIEVE IT. HOW IS THAT EVEN POSSIBLE?!

DO YOU REMEMBER WHAT THAT SKELETON, BROOK, SAID?

HE SAID HIS SHADOW WAS STOLEN FROM HIM! SO DID THAT GUY DO IT?

RM RM RM...

??

SKRNK
SKRNK

I BET HE'LL TAKE ME ANOTHER STEP CLOSER TO BECOMING THE PIRATE KING.

KI SHI SHI!!!

HOGBACK!!

WHEN THAT SHADOW IS INSERTED, IT WILL PRODUCE THE GREATEST ZOMBIE OF ALL TIME. WE WILL HAVE TREMENDOUS POWER!

FOHO
FOHO

I PUT EVERYTHING I HAD INTO THE CREATION OF NUMBER 900. I'VE BEEN WORKING TOWARD THIS DAY EVER SINCE WE MET TEN YEARS AGO.

MY DREAM OF CREATING MY OWN KINGDOM FULL OF OBEDIENT SERFS IS ONE STEP CLOSER!!

*I'LL* TAKE EVERYTHING CUTE IN THE WORLD AND MAKE THEM INTO ZOMBIES!

...THE CEMETERY KING OF THE ENTIRE WORLD!!

THAT MEANS THE DAY IS CLOSE THAT I'LL BECOME...

WITH THIS MANY UNDERLINGS...

...I WOULDN'T HAVE LOST TO THAT IDIOT KAIDO IN THE NEW WORLD THE WAY I DID LAST TIME!

THAT'S RIGHT! NO MATTER HOW DEFIANT A PERSON IS, THEIR SHADOWS ARE OBEDIENT TO ME! THE ENTIRE WORLD WILL BE POPULATED WITH OBEDIENT ZOMBIES!

OPEN THE GATE TO THE SPECIAL FREEZER!!

900

LET'S WAKE IT UP! KI SHI SHI!!

YES, MASTER!

GYORO! NIN! BAO!

WHAT?

BUT PLEASE WAIT-- THERE IS SOMETHING TO REPORT!

YES, SIR!

SPIDER MICE, GO DUMP STRAW HAT LUFFY'S ORIGINAL ON HIS SHIP.

DON'T FORGET TO UNTIE HIM. WE DON'T WANT HIM TO DIE.

BWONG!!

BONG

IT'S NOT LIKE HE COULD'VE HAD HIS SHADOW REMOVED.

DEFEATED HOW?

NOT LONG AGO, CAPTAIN "SPIDER MONKEY" TARALAN WAS DEFEATED!

...

ABSALOM, THERE'S ONLY ONE MAN I KNOW WHO CAN DO THAT!

?!

HIS SHADOW WAS REMOVED!!

IT SEEMS THE NIGHTMARE OF FIVE YEARS AGO HAS BEGUN TO REPEAT ITSELF!!!

AND THERE ARE NUMEROUS OTHER VICTIMS!

...

THE CULPRIT IS THAT HUMMING SWORDSMAN!!

YOU DON'T KNOW WHAT HE LOOKS LIKE?!

PERONA!

I'VE HEARD ABOUT HIM, BUT WHAT IS HE LIKE?

CURSE IT ALL. HE'S THE ONLY ONE WHO HAS FIGURED OUT THE ZOMBIES' WEAKNESS.

THAT MEANS HE COULD'VE SLIPPED BY YOU DURING YOUR RECON.

CINDRY! WHY ARE YOU STANDING IN FRONT OF ME?!

HOW DID HE FIND OUT? AND HOW DID HE END UP BACK HERE?!

YOU DO SOMETHING ABOUT IT.

I DON'T CARE. IT'S NOT MY PROBLEM.

MASTER, IT SEEMS WE HAVE ANOTHER SOURCE OF TROUBLE ON THE ISLAND!

NOW, LET'S GET GOING TO THE FREEZER.

W-WAIT!

NOW HURRY UP AND DUMP STRAW HAT BACK ON HIS SHIP!

IF ANOTHER PROBLEM ARISES, REPORT BACK TO ME.

YOU FOOL. YOU SHOULD'VE TOLD ME THAT FIRST.

BUT RIGHT NOW...

HUPP

HUPP

UNDER-STOOD!!

Sn ar!!

GAH!

THEN ALL WE NEED TO DO IS HOLD HIM AT BAY.

WHSP

....!

LUFFY!!!

HEY! STAY INSIDE!

HUPP

HUPP

THEY'RE GOING TO DO SOMETHING WITH LUFFY'S SHADOW.

WE CAN'T GO OUT RIGHT NOW!

IT'S THE SAME AS BROOK.

I DON'T THINK HE'LL DIE, EVEN IF HIS SHADOW IS TAKEN AWAY.

ZUP

WE NEED TO SEE JUST WHAT THEY DO SO WE CAN GET IT BACK LATER!

WE NEED TO WAIT FOR THE RIGHT OPPORTUNITY!

...

WHERE ARE THOSE TWO?!

WHERE DID THEY GO?!

THEY'RE NOT HERE!

BETWEEN MAST MANSION AND HOGBACK'S MANSION MEZZANINE LEVEL

SPIDER WEB PASSAGE-WAY

WHERE IS THE ENEMY?! I WANT TO CUT SOMEONE!!

I DIDN'T THINK TARALAN WOULD LOSE!!

YOUR SONG

DOOM!!

TMP TMP...

INSIDE GECKO MORIA'S MAST MANSION

AUGH!!!

OF COURSE.

HUFF    HUFF

SO YOU WON'T GIVE UP EVEN IF I PUSH YOU OFF THE SIDE.

YO HO HO HO, I KNEW IT.

SILENCE! YOU ARE MY SHADOW!!

ALL WILL COWER IN FEAR WHEN THEY HEAR THE NAME OF THE SWORDMASTER RYUMA...

DON'T YOU KNOW MY NAME?!

MARIO COO

KLUNK!!

...RETURN TO MY FEET!

I WILL HAVE YOU...

THE FUNDAMENTAL STRENGTHS OF OUR BODIES ARE COMPLETELY DIFFERENT!

YO HO HO HO...

I CAN'T WAIT!

THE NATIONS THAT FELL AT HIS HANDS WERE TAKEN WHOLE, ISLAND AND EVERYTHING...

I COULD NOT BELIEVE THAT SOMETHING SO FEARSOME WREAKED HAVOC IN THE SEAS 500 YEARS AGO!

...I COULDN'T STOP TREMBLING.

UPON FINDING HIS CORPSE IN THE LAND OF ICE...

...AND HE CREATED A NATION OF VILLAINS.

IT'S SO COLD!

THE ONE WHO CREATED THE FAMOUS LEGEND OF THE CONTINENT PULLER WAS RIGHT BEFORE MY EYES!

IN ALL OF HISTORY, YOU ARE THE ONLY ONE KNOWN AS...

SLAM!!

NOW! IT IS TIME FOR YOUR REVIVAL!!

ANOTHER LEGEND WILL BE REVIVED! KI SHI SHI!!

THIS IS WHAT MAKES ZOMBIE CREATION SO WORTHWHILE.

# Chapter 457: MEAT!!!

...

SLUMP...

I AM YOUR NEW MASTER!

SKRNK

CALM DOWN, SHADOW OF STRAW HAT LUFFY!

SKRNK

YOU WILL FORGET ALL HUMAN RELATIONSHIPS YOU HAD IN THE PAST...

...AND BECOME MY LOYAL SOLDIER!!

I WILL NOW PROVIDE YOU A VOICE AND BODY...

...SO YOU CAN LIVE ON AS MY ZOMBIE.

...!!

KI SHI SHI! THE PACT HAS BEEN SEALED!!

NOD ...!!

KI SHI SHI!

WHAT?

LUFFY'S SHADOW JUST...

...IT'S IN!!

KRINK KRANK...

?!!

RRRM
M
M
B
B
B
B

RMM
SKREE
BB
SKREE
FLAP FLAP

BA-BUMP...

KRINK
KLANK

BA-BUMP...

...

HMM? WHO'S SANJI?!

SANJI! FOOD!!

OHH...

YOU WON'T GET AWAY FROM ME!!

THEY RAN AWAY AT FULL SPEED!

GONE IN THE BLINK OF AN EYE!

HEY! WHERE DID THE PIRATES GO?!

?!

...DR. HOGBACK TALKED ABOUT REVIVING...

SO THAT'S WHAT HE MEANT! THOSE ZOMBIES...

HUFF... HUFF... WHEN LUFFY'S SHADOW WAS PUT INTO THAT THING, IT STARTED MOVING!!

HUFF! WHAT WAS THAT? WHAT WAS GOING ON BACK THERE?!

THAT HUGE MAN HAS HUGE POWERS! IT MUST BE THE POWER OF THE DEVIL FRUIT!

HUFF

HUFF

HUFF

TMP TMP TMP

TMP TMP TMP

HUFF

GAH...!!

KOFF...

WHAT?!

OW!! LET GO OF ME!!!

...?!

FWOP FWOP

WUPWUPWUP

USOPP! CHOPPER!!

...!!!

DO YOU WANT TO SAY GOODBYE?

THIS WOMAN IS GOING TO MARRY ME TODAY.

HE'S SO STRONG!

!!!

Q: What's Franky's Jolly Roger like?

--Sen-chan

A: Well, I suppose everyone has their own Jolly Roger
◄ How's this?

Q: I have a question! Swordmaster Ryuma, who is said to have defeated a dragon, is the same person as the main character Ryuma in your *Wanted!* short story "Monsters," right? This bothers me so much that I can't even brush my teeth. If I get a cavity, I'm going to tell the dentist, "It's Mr. Oda's fault."

--Tomopyon

Q: Nice to meet you! I was reading "Romance Dawn" in *Wanted!* recently and I get the feeling that Luffy's grandfather in the story has to be Vice Admiral Garp. If that's true, does it mean Vice Admiral Garp used to be the captain of a band of pirates?

--NAO

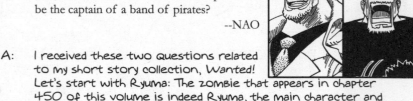

A: I received these two questions related to my short story collection, Wanted! Let's start with Ryuma: The zombie that appears in chapter 450 of this volume is indeed Ryuma, the main character and samurai in the short story "Monsters." In the world of One Piece, he has already died from an illness and is revered as a legendary swordsman. I could have just ignored this matter, but I was really happy to see how many people noticed it. As for the second question, about Garp, the one-shot comic was a prototype for One Piece and Luffy's grandfather appeared as a pirate. He looks identical, but please think of them as different people. The Garp in One Piece has been a bona fide navy man all his life.

# Chapter 458:
# ANYTHING BUT
# MY AFRO

**ENERU'S GREAT SPACE MISSION, VOL. 24: "DIVINE JUDGMENT"**

OHHH, NO...

THIS IS ROTTEN HORRIBLE. "WE CAN'T DIE" WAS PRACTICALLY OUR MOTTO.

I DON'T WANT TO BE AFRAID OF DYING AGAIN!

BUZZ BUZZ

...THAT HUMMING SWORDSMAN WHO KNOW ABOUT OUR WEAKNESS?

ARE THERE PEOPLE OTHER THAN...

YEAH, LUFFY WAS TAKEN DOWN HERE TOO!!

WE WERE CHASING AFTER HIM AND SUDDENLY NAMI...

...WAS THE PASSAGE THEY USED TO CARRY PEOPLE WHOSE SHADOWS HAD BEEN CUT.

TMP
TMP
T

I HEARD THIS LARGE STAIRWAY...

WHAT WAS THAT MONSTER-LIKE GROANING I HEARD UP THERE?

WE WENT RIGHT TO YOU AFTER HEARING THAT.

WE'LL HAVE TO START FRESH, BUT WE'LL DEFINITELY RESCUE HER!

THEY'RE NOT TRYING TO KILL HER.

I WONDER IF NAMI IS OKAY.

I'LL TELL YOU EVERYTHING.

?!

THAT'S LUFFY'S VOICE.

...TMP TMP TMP

RM RM RM

...WE'VE GOT A TERRIBLE SITUATION ON OUR HANDS!

ANYWAY...

RM RM...

BUT IT'S DANGEROUS FOR ME WHEN THE SUN IS UP...

...AND IT'LL BE EASIER FOR THE ENEMY TO FIND ME TOO.

HUFF... HUFF... I'M SCARED OF ZOMBIES.

IT'S ESPECIALLY BAD AT NIGHT!

AWOOO...

NOW IF I RUN REALLY FAST TO MAKE SURE I CAN'T SEE THEIR FACES...

...AND PURIFY EACH ONE...

OH, IT'S JUST A GRASS-HOPPER.

AH! THAT SCARED ME!

BA-BUMP!!

I-I KNOW! I'LL KEEP MY MIND OCCUPIED BY SINGING!

AHHHHHH!

IS SOMEONE HUMMING?!

WHAT'S THAT SONG?

...I'LL EVENTUALLY FIND MY SHADOW!

AHHHHHH!

AHHHHHHH!

HMMMM... HUMM...

SWIP SWIP

GAAAAH

WHO'S THERE?!!

ZWIP

...BUT I CAN'T KEEP UP WITH HIM AT ALL!

YO HO HO.

HIS SWORD FIGHTING STYLE IS THE SAME AS MINE...

...SUP-POSED TO BE ME?!

WHAT IS THIS POWER? ISN'T THIS ZOMBIE...

W-WHAT?! NO!!!

?!

...SO YOU CAN MOVE A LITTLE FASTER.

I SHOULD CUT OFF THAT BIG AFRO OF YOURS...

PLEASE DON'T TOUCH MY AFRO!!

GIVE UP.

IT'LL BE THE SAME NO MATTER HOW MANY TIMES YOU TRY ME

...IS YELLING AND WREAKING HAVOC!

LUFFY'S ZOMBIE...

HUFF

...AND THE LOUD ROAR CAME FROM THE SAME GUY!!

THAT HUGE SOUND YOU HEARD...

WE'D BETTER HURRY!

HUFF

DIDN'T THINK THOSE STEPS WOULD GO STRAIGHT UP TO THE BOSSES ROOM!

SO THIS IS WHERE IT LEADS TO...

THERE'S SUNNY!!

THRILLER BARK

IT'S MADE SO THAT THEY CAN LAY ON THE STEPS.

IT'S THOSE ZOMBIES.

THEY LEFT MUDDY FOOTPRINTS EVERYWHERE.

WHAT?! THEN MAYBE THEY'RE STILL HERE!

WHAT A MESS!!

BUT WHERE ARE THE THREE WE'RE LOOKING FOR?

I DON'T SEE THEM ANYWHERE.

IT'S NOT LIKE WE HAVE ANYTHING WORTH STEALING RIGHT NOW.

THEY REALLY DID MAKE A MESS, *AND* THEY TRIED TO GO THROUGH OUR STUFF.

ARE THERE Z-ZOMBIES HERE?

ALL THREE OF THEM!

I FOUND THEM! THEY'RE IN THE DINING ROOM!

SANJI!!

ZOLO!!

HEY! LUFFY!!

THEY LOOK MISERABLE.

THE ZOMBIES DID 'EM UP.

OUT OF THE WAY. I'LL USE MY BAZOOKA.

CAN'T THEY FEEL ANYTHING?

THEY'RE NOT WAKING UP...

...

NO, I KNOW WHAT TO DO...

HEY, ALL OF YOU! WAKE UP! THIS IS NO TIME TO BE SLEEPING!!!

WE GOT A SERIOUS PROBLEM ON OUR HANDS!

SMAK!!!

SMASH!!! KRAK!!! POW!!

LOOK, THERE'S A BEAUTIFUL FEMALE SWORD MASTER CARRYING LOTS OF MEAT!!!

Q: Oda Sensei, there's something that's bothering me! The way the Navy and Koby are saluting seems to be different from what I know. Don't you usually place your hand directly perpendicular to your forehead? Please tell me!

--Soyatte

A: Oh, right. It might be a little late, but I guess I never answered this before. You're right that this salute is a bit different from the usual one, but there is a reason for it. The crew of a sailing ship needs to pull a lot of  ropes in order to steer it. There's tar on the ropes, so their palms are usually completely blackened. It's considered rude to show those blackened hands to an officer who outranks you, so they hide their palms when saluting. It's all based on Navy etiquette.

Q: Hello, Oda Sensei. I came up with this question while I was watching a daytime talk show. I see this in other pieces of work as well as *One Piece*, but what do they mean when they say "so and so at 9 o'clock or 12 o'clock?"

--〇〇〇 Behind You

A: Assume that you're standing on the center of a clock and you're facing the number 12. That would mean that 6 o'clock is directly behind you. You don't have to worry about north/south/east/west. It just tells you the direction relative to the ship.

Q: Hello, Odacchi. *One Piece* started when I was in the first grade, but when I learned that it will be celebrating its 10th anniversary, I counted all the panels up to volume 45. After doing this  research over the course of two months, I have confirmed that it is 40,971 panels! (Applause)... *Crickets* L-let's go for the 100,000th panel next! I'll come again when you get to your 500th chapter. Bye-bye baby! Ha! Spin! Crash!

--Mr. Nine's Best Student Tatsuya

A: Thanks for counting. So I drew more than 40,000 panels. Hmm. It just doesn't seem real. But I will thank you for the amount of effort you put in! Thank you! See you in the Question Corner next volume!

# Chapter 459:
# I CAN'T JUST DIE HOPING TO BE FORGIVEN

ENERU'S GREAT SPACE MISSION, VOL. 25:
"THE HELPLESS SPACE PIRATE"

SORRY! BUT IT WASN'T REALLY POSSIBLE FOR US TO GO AFTER HER!

I'LL EXPLAIN EVERYTHING NOW!

SHE WAS KIDNAPPED?! WHY DIDN'T YOU FOLLOW HER TO THE ENDS OF THE EARTH?!!

WHO KIDNAPPED HER?! I'LL GO AND GET HER BACK RIGHT NOW!!!

UH... I REALLY DIDN'T THINK ONE OF THOSE WOULD MAKE THE LIST. ANYWAY, LET ME TALK ABOUT NAMI AND THE SHADOWS FIRST.

AND SHADOWS. THAT'S *THREE*.

NAMI!!

MEAT!!

LISTEN! RIGHT NOW, THERE ARE TWO THINGS THAT WE HAVE TO GET BACK!

WHAT?!

M-MAA --!!

RM RM

RM RM

RM..

SO YOU ALREADY SAW LUFFY AND THE COOK'S ZOMBIES?

SO I'M A GIANT... AND THAT'S HOW ZOMBIES ARE MADE?

HE WANTS TO MARRY NAMI? THAT GUY'S GOT SOME GUTS.

I WON'T LET IT HAPPEN!!

GETTING MARRIED?! THAT'S BULL!!

BWOOF

USOPP.

...I KNOW WHO YOUR ZOMBIE IS, ZOLO.

HM? OH, RIGHT. SO IF THE ZOMBIES BECOME LIKE THE ACTUAL PERSON...

YOU DIDN'T KNOW?

NOW I'M SCARED!!

I DIDN'T KNOW HE WAS ONE OF THE SEVEN WARLORDS!

TRMB  TRMB  TRMB

TRMB

SO IF WE FIND THOSE THREE ZOMBIES AND PUT SALT IN THEIR MOUTHS...

WHATEVER.

...OUR SHADOWS WILL COME BACK?

HE WAS KIND OF LIKE YOU. BUT HE WORE WOODEN CLOGS.

WHAT'S HE LIKE?

I KNEW RIGHT AWAY IT WASN'T YOU.

WHAT?! YOU SAW BROOK?!

...ADVISED US TO COME BACK HERE FIRST.

IT WAS THAT SKELETON WHO TOLD US ABOUT THE WEAKNESS AND...

I'M SURPRISED YOU FOUND THAT WEAKNESS.

GRR GRR

...BUT ONCE YOU GET TO TALK TO HIM...

Y'KNOW, THAT SKELETON MAY BE SKINNY AND EVERYTHING...

WELL, WHEN YOU FIRST BROUGHT HIM HERE AND SAID YOU WANTED HIM TO JOIN US...

I SAW HIM, AND I ASKED HIM A VERY INSENSITIVE QUESTION.

I DID...

...I COMPLETELY DENIED HIS EXISTENCE.

...

BECAUSE HE'S A SKELETON.

...YOU FIND OUT THAT HE'S GOT A REAL BACKBONE.

YOU MIGHT AS WELL ANSWER ONE MORE QUESTION.

WAIT JUST A SECOND!

BUT HE'S A REAL MAN!!!

...WILL BE ABLE TO MAKE ANY FRIENDS. PEOPLE WHO LOOK THAT DIFFERENT FROM OTHERS WILL ALWAYS BE CAST ASIDE!!

YOU'RE A TALKING SKELETON. THERE'S NO WAY SOMEONE AS CREEPY AS YOU...

?!

...YOU KNOW WHAT PEOPLE'S REACTIONS WILL BE.

IF YOU GO OUT IN PUBLIC LOOKING LIKE THAT...

FRANKY, WHAT ARE YOU SAYING?

...

YOU SAID YOURSELF THAT YOU WERE SO LONELY YOU WANTED TO DIE.

KREAK... KREAK...

EVEN IF YOU MANAGED TO ESCAPE THESE DEMONIC WATERS, YOUR FATE IS CLEAR.

IF I WERE YOU, I WOULD HAVE KILLED MYSELF A LONG TIME AGO!!!

NOT TO MENTION THE DECADES YOU SPENT HERE IN DESPAIR.

WHAT IS IT THAT'S KEEPING YOU ALIVE?

YOUR ENTIRE EXISTENCE IS FRAGILE, YET YOU STILL ACT LIKE A GENTLEMAN.

...

WHAT IS THAT PACT WITH A FRIEND YOU NEED TO FULFILL?!

YOU ALWAYS COVER UP YOUR PROBLEMS WHEN TALKING TO US TOO!

...AT SOME POINT IN THE PAST.

IT WAS A TROUBLING SEPARATION, BUT WE DID IT OUT OF NECESSITY.

IT'S VERY SIMPLE...

WE LEFT BEHIND A FRIEND OF OUR PIRATE CREW...

YOU LIKE TO MEDDLE IN OTHER PEOPLE'S BUSINESS, I SEE.

YO HO HO...

AND OUR BAND OF PIRATES DIED OFF IN THESE WATERS...

...LEAVING THAT PROMISE UNFULFILLED...

WE SET SAIL AFTER WE PROMISED TO...

...RETURN AT ALL COSTS.

IT HAS PROBABLY BEEN 50 YEARS SINCE THE DAY WE DIED.

...TO RETURN AND TELL HIM ABOUT THIS!

BECAUSE I AM THE ONLY ONE WHO SURVIVED FROM THE SHIP, IT IS MY DUTY...

...

I BELIEVE THAT HE WOULD BE VERY BIG BY NOW!!!

BWOOO!!!

YEAAAH!

WE'LL DEFINITELY BE BACK!

HE WAS STILL A BABY WHALE AT THE TIME, AND WE COULDN'T TAKE HIM WITH US ON SUCH A DANGEROUS VOYAGE.

...PLAYING OUR USUAL CHEERFUL MUSIC.

BWOOO!!

HE MAY EVEN STILL BELIEVE WE WILL RETURN...

I CAN'T SHAKE OFF THE FEELING THAT HE STILL THINKS OF US.

THAT'S RIGHT.

YOUR FRIEND IS A *WHALE*?!

...I CAN'T JUST DIE HOPING TO BE FORGIVEN!

KLNCH...!!

...BUT AFTER COERCING HIM INTO AGREEING TO SUCH A SELFISH PACT, ONE THAT WE ENDED UP BEING UNABLE TO FULFILL IN THIS FARAWAY PLACE...

I DON'T THINK HE WILL FORGIVE US FOR DYING SO IRRESPONSIBLY...

BECAUSE WHEN A MAN PROMISES TO RETURN, HE MUST RETURN!!!

LABOON.

THAT'S WHY HE...

...

...!!

OH.

HIM?

ARE YOU SERIOUS?

IT'S HIM.

...

WHAT?! WHAT DO YOU MEAN?!

...

**BWOOO**

IN THE ENTRANCE TO THE GRAND LINE...

...THERE'S A PLACE CALLED THE TWIN CAPE.

THERE'S A DARNED HUGE WHALE THERE...

...AND HE WAS RAMMING HIS HEAD AGAINST THE WALL THAT SEPARATES THE WORLD.

...

HE'S STILL WAITING FOR THE PIRATES WHO MADE A PROMISE TO HIM 50 YEARS AGO... VOWING THAT...

...THEY WOULD RETURN.

...BUT HE'S STILL ALIVE AND WAITING FOR HIS FRIEND AT THAT CAPE!

LUFFY MANAGED TO STOP LABOON FROM KILLING HIMSELF BY RAMMING HIS HEAD ON THE RED LINE...

...LABOON REFUSED TO ACCEPT THAT AND CONTINUED TO HOWL.

THERE WAS SOME SUGGESTION THAT THE PIRATES HAD ALREADY FLED FROM THE GRAND LINE, BUT...

BWOOO

K
L
A
N
K

I NEVER EXPECTED THAT ONE OF THE PIRATES LABOON WAS WAITING FOR...

THIS IS GREAT! THEY BOTH KEPT THEIR PROMISE FOR OVER 50 YEARS!

SHWANK!

HUFF

HUFF

...WAS...

...THAT SKELETON.

SH

ANK!!

KLANKKA!!

AAH!

...IT'S ALL THE SAME TO ME!

EVEN IF YOU HAVE BECOME STRONGER OVER THE LAST FIVE YEARS...

YO HO HO HO!

FWUP

SHWAK!

THE WAY WE THINK IS EXACTLY THE SAME!

!

HUFF

...

HUFF

KRUSH!

AGH!

HUFF

THERE IS NO WAY YOU CAN DEFEND SUCH A LARGE WEAK POINT!

YOHOHO

YOU SEEM TO CARE A GREAT DEAL ABOUT YOUR AFRO, AS ALWAYS!

I HAVE NOTHING LEFT OF MY OLD SELF...

HUFF

HUFF

AH! STOP! NOT MY AFRO!

...YOU PROBABLY WOULDN'T EVEN RECOGNIZE ME, BECAUSE I'VE TURNED INTO A SKELETON.

IF WE WERE TO MEET AGAIN...

SHWAK!!

ZWIP!

KLANK!!

YO HO HO!

AHHHH!

THIS IS THE ONLY TRACE OF ME YOU MAY STILL RECOGNIZE! I WILL PROTECT IT WITH MY LIFE!

BWOOOO♪

...BUT THIS SMALL THING...

...THIS HEAD OF HAIR THAT EVERYONE LAUGHED AT, SAYING IT LOOKED LIKE LABOON!

KR!!!AK!!

I WILL COME SEE YOU!

WAIT FOR ME... AT THE CAPE WHERE WE MADE OUR PACT!!!

GEEZ, WOULD YA SHUT UP ?!!

I LOVE BOTH THE SKELETON AND THE WHALE!

WAAAAGH!!

FLOOSH

I'M GOING TO MAKE HIM JOIN OUR CREW EVEN IF I HAVE TO FORCE HIM!

HE'S JOINING US! ANYONE GOT A PROBLEM WITH THAT?!

HAHA! NOW I'M GETTING EXCITED! HE'S A MUSICIAN!

HE'S A TALKING SKELETON! HE HAS AN AFRO! HE GOES "YO HO HO!" AND HE'S LABOON'S FRIEND!

ME TOO! I'M NOT SCARED OF SKELETONS ANYMORE!

I'M WITH YOU, BROS!

I REALLY WANT TO GET HIM AND LABOON TO SEE EACH OTHER AGAIN!

HA HA.

EVEN IF WE DID, WOULD ANYTHING CHANGE YOUR MIND?

KAAAAA

TO BE CONTINUED IN ONE PIECE, VOL. 48!

 COLORING PAGE

SEE INTO THE SOUL
OF *BLEACH*
WITH THE MANGA,
PROFILES AND ART BOOKS

# The mystery behind *manga-making* revealed!

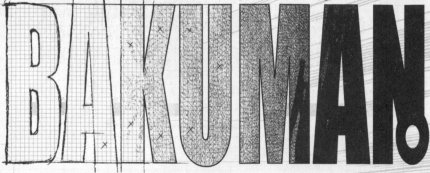

*Story by* **TSUGUMI OHBA** — *Art by* **TAKESHI OBATA**

From the creators of **Death Note**

**BAKUMAN** COMPLETE BOX SET Volumes 1–20

Comes with a *two-sided poster* and the *Otter No. 11* mini-comic!

Average student Moritaka Mashiro enjoys drawing for fun. When his classmate and aspiring writer Akito Takagi discovers his talent, he begs Moritaka to team up with him as a manga-creating duo. But what exactly does it take to make it in the manga-publishing world?

## This *bestselling series* is now available in a COMPLETE BOX SET!

**A 20% SAVINGS OVER BUYING THE INDIVIDUAL VOLUMES!**

# BAKUMAN.

STORY BY TSUGUMI OHBA
ART BY TAKESHI OBATA

From the creators of *Death Note*

## The mystery behind manga making REVEALED!

Average student Moritaka Mashiro enjoys drawing for fun. When his classmate and aspiring writer Akito Takagi discovers his talent, he begs to team up. But what exactly does it take to make it in the manga-publishing world?

Bakuman, Vol. 1
ISBN: 978-1-4215-3513-5
$9.99 US / $12.99 CAN *

# You're Reading in the Wrong Direction!!

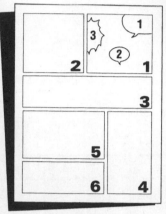

**W**hoops! Guess what? You're starting at the wrong end of the comic!

...It's true! In keeping with the original Japanese format, **One Piece** is meant to be read from right to left, starting in the upper-right corner.

Unlike English, which is read from left to right, Japanese is read from right to left, meaning that action, sound effects and word-balloon order are completely reversed...something which can make readers unfamiliar with Japanese feel pretty backwards themselves. For this reason, manga or Japanese comics published in the U.S. in English have sometimes been published "flopped"— that is, printed in exact reverse order, as though seen from the other side of a mirror.

By flopping pages, U.S. publishers can avoid confusing readers, but the compromise is not without its downside. For one thing, a character in a flopped manga series who once wore in the original Japanese version a T-shirt emblazoned with "M A Y" (as in "the merry month of") now wears one which reads "Y A M"! Additionally, many manga creators in Japan are themselves unhappy with the process, as some feel the mirror-imaging of their art skews their original intentions.

We are proud to bring you Eiichiro Oda's **One Piece** in the original unflopped format. For now, though, turn to the other side of the book and let the journey begin...!

—Editor